UNDEAD PETS

GASP OF THE GHOULISH GUINEA PIG

For my supercool nephews Quinten and Elliot—SH

For Gizmo, our fine, furry friend—SC

GROSSET & DUNLAP
Penguin Young Readers Group
An Imprint of Penguin Random House LLC

Text copyright © 2014 by Sam Hay. Illustrations copyright © 2014 by Simon Cooper. All rights reserved.
First printed in Great Britain in 2014 by Stripes Publishing. First published in the United States of America
in 2016 by Grosset & Dunlap, an imprint of Penguin Random House LLC, 345 Hudson Street, New York,
New York 10014. GROSSET & DUNLAP is a trademark of Penguin Random House LLC. Printed in the USA.

Library of Congress Cataloging-in-Publication Data is available.

ISBN 978-0-448-49003-8   10 9 8 7 6 5 4 3 2 1

UNDEAD PETS

GASP OF THE GHOULISH GUINEA PIG

by Sam Hay
illustrated by Simon Cooper

Grosset & Dunlap
An Imprint of Penguin Random House

The story so far . . .

Ten-year-old Joe Edmunds is desperate for a pet.

But his mom's allergies mean that he's got no chance.

Then his great-uncle Charlie gives him an ancient Egyptian amulet that he claims will grant Joe a single wish . . .

But instead of getting a pet, Joe becomes the Protector of Undead Pets.
He is bound by the amulet to solve the problems of zombie pets so
they can pass peacefully to the afterlife.

And so the trouble begins . . .

CHAPTER ONE

"Here they come!" called Joe.

Toby, his little brother, gave a squeal of delight as a streak of brown-and-white fur shot out of a bendy green tube, closely followed by two more.

"Go, guinea pigs!" shouted Erin, a curly-haired girl the same age as Joe. She was sitting at the other end of the hall waving a bunch of parsley, while three guinea pigs raced through the obstacle course toward her, squeaking as they went.

UNDEAD PETS

It was Sunday afternoon, the start of winter break, and Joe and Toby and their parents were visiting the Crawfords. While the grown-ups chatted in the living room, the children were playing with the family's three guinea pigs—Lightning, Flash, and Bolt. The obstacle course they'd built ran down the length of the Crawfords' hallway.

"Oops!" George, Erin's little brother, giggled as the guinea pigs decided not to jump over the small fence the kids had made and went around the side instead.

"They're heading for the seesaw!" shrieked Toby.

"Come on!" called Erin, waving the parsley up and down. "Come and get the goodies!"

Flash—the biggest guinea pig—sniffed the air and let out a squeak, then shot through the cardboard archway and over the finish line, closely followed by Bolt and Lightning.

UNDEAD PETS

"Why does Flash always win?" groaned George.

"Because he's awesome!" Erin gently scooped up Flash and rewarded him with a sprig of parsley. "That's why I chose him."

"Lightning and Bolt are cool, too," said George, giving the other two their share of the parsley.

Joe crouched down next to Erin and stroked Flash's small brown-and-white head. "When did you get them?"

"About four months ago. They're still pretty young . . ."

"And very excitable!" added Erin's mom, who had appeared in the hall carrying a tray of empty mugs. "All that squeaking!"

"Squeak! Squeak!" mimicked George in a funny guinea-pig voice.

Toby laughed and joined in. "Squeak! Squeak! Squeak!"

The guinea pigs stopped chewing their parsley and looked at the boys as though they were upset.

"I wish I had a guinea pig." Toby sighed. "They're so cool."

"Want to hold Flash?" Erin nodded to the spot next to her. "Sit there and I'll put him on your lap. Watch out—he's a bit of a pooper!"

Toby and George giggled.

"Can I hold one, too?" Joe asked.

George put Bolt on Joe's knee. The guinea pig began snuffling around the boy's pockets looking for treats. Joe stroked his head and the guinea pig gave a small squeak.

"He likes you," said Erin.

But just then Bolt wriggled off Joe's lap and scuttled back to Lightning.

"They're best friends," George explained. "They like to stick together."

"What about Flash?" asked Joe. The biggest guinea pig was still sitting happily on Toby's knee.

"He's a bit braver," said Erin. "The other two follow him around. It's a bit like me and George." She giggled. "I'm Flash, and George is Bolt!"

"Joe, Toby—five minutes!" Mom called from the living room.

Toby groaned. "I don't want to go home!"

"Quick," Erin said. "Let's do the course again!" She picked up Flash and Lightning, while George took Bolt. They carried them back to the beginning of the obstacle course.

UNDEAD PETS

As soon as Erin let Flash go, he took off through the first tunnel, squeaking excitedly.

"Hey!" said Erin, as Lightning wriggled in her arms. She put him down, and he chased after Flash. Bolt caught up, following the others.

George and Toby began squeaking again, copying the guinea pigs.

"We've got two new pets!" said Mrs. Crawford as the grown-ups appeared in the hall.

Joe's dad grinned. "Should I put them in the hutch for you?"

START

UNDEAD PETS

Toby and George made silly guinea-pig faces and squeaked even louder.

"Come on, boys! Time to go," said Mom, holding out Toby's fleece.

Toby's face fell. "But I want to stay."

"You can come back another time," said Mrs. Crawford. "What about Tuesday? It's George's birthday, and he's having a monster party. He'd love if Joe and Toby could come."

"Yes, please!" said Toby excitedly.

"Cool!" George added.

Joe was less excited. The idea of a five-year-old's birthday party wasn't so appealing to him.

"Well . . . ," he began.

Mrs. Crawford smiled. "Maybe you've already got plans, Joe. But it would be nice if Toby could come."

"Are you sure you don't mind?" Mom asked Mrs. Crawford.

"Of course not! We've already got a houseful of kids coming—another one won't matter."

"Awesome!" said Toby and George. And they started squeaking again.

"Five more minutes, Joe, and then knock it off!" called Dad, poking his head through the living-room door.

It was a few hours later, and Joe was playing a racing video game.

"Did you hear me?" Joe's dad asked.

Joe made a face. "Yeah, all right, Dad."

Just one more lap, he thought as he steered his car through the flags.

Squeak! Squeak! Squeak!

"Get lost, Toby!" Joe grumbled, not bothering to turn around. "Dad says I've still got five minutes!"

Squeak! Squeak! Squeak!

UNDEAD PETS

"Go away!"

Squeak! Squeak! Squeak!

Why were little brothers so annoying! Joe grabbed a cushion, spun around, and lobbed it at Toby—but he wasn't there.

Squeak! Squeak! Squeak!

Joe frowned. "Toby? Where are you?"

"Under here, Joe!" came a squeaky voice.

Joe looked under the coffee table and gasped. It was Flash!

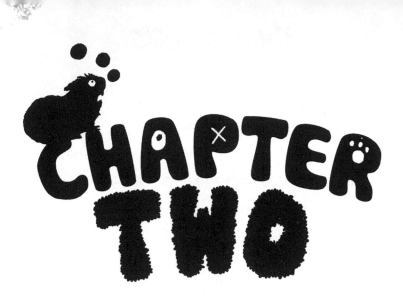

CHAPTER TWO

Joe blinked a few times. It really *was* Flash. But the guinea pig looked different than the super-sleek blur of fur that had been zooming around the obstacle course at the Crawfords' house earlier that day.

Flash's coat was damp. His eyes were big, green, and bulging. And every time he opened his mouth, little soapy bubbles popped out.

Joe rubbed his eyes.

"I need your help!" said Flash urgently, and an extra big bubble popped out of his nose, filling the room with a flowery smell.

Joe gulped. "Are you . . . uh . . . dead?"

"I can't pass over properly until you help me!"

Joe groaned. Flash had become an Undead Pet: another creature unable to pass over to the afterlife until his problems had been solved. And thanks to the magical Egyptian amulet that Joe's great-uncle Charlie had given him, there was only one person who could help—Joe!

"But, how . . . ?" Joe muttered. "I was playing with you a few hours ago!"

"A lot has happened since you left," the guinea pig said miserably.

Just then there was a shout from upstairs.

"Come on, Joe," called Dad. "Turn it off now!"

"Okay, coming!" Joe shut off his game and turned back to Flash. "What happened to you?"

Flash trotted out from under the table, leaving a trail of damp footprints on the carpet. "It's a long story . . ."

The guinea pig gave himself a shake, splattering Joe with sweet-smelling droplets.

"Ugh! What's that smell? Did you pour a bottle of perfume over your head or something?"

"It's fabric softener," said Flash.

"What?"

"You know—the gloopy stuff that goes in the washing machine." As Flash spoke, a ripple of bubbles escaped from his nose.

"But how did you get covered in it?"

"After you left, George and Erin put us back in our hutch, but I wanted to keep playing. I noticed that George hadn't shut the hutch properly . . ."

"So you got out?" Joe asked.

Flash nodded. "I ran through the kitchen, but then something horrible appeared!" He began to shiver, and a big bubble burst out of his left nostril.

"What was it?"

"A snake!" Flash let out a squeal.

"Very funny!" Joe rolled his eyes.

"No, really. There was a snake in the kitchen!" Flash's fur was standing on end now, and his eyes bulged even more. "It was huge. A monster!"

Joe frowned. "But Erin and George don't have a snake."

"I saw it!" squeaked Flash.

"Okay," Joe said, going along with the story, although he found it hard to believe. "What did you do?"

I froze. I was terrified!

Then I ran! I noticed a pile of clothes next to the washing machine.

I climbed up and dived inside . . .

But then Mom came in. She didn't see me.

She stuffed the clothes inside the machine and turned it on!

Joe winced. "You drowned?"

Flash nodded. "Look at me!"

A few more bubbles drifted out of the damp guinea pig's mouth and floated toward Joe, who popped them. "So, what do you need me for?"

"To save my friends from the snake! What if it eats Bolt and Lightning?"

"But maybe it wasn't a snake," Joe said. "I mean, snakes don't just magically appear in kitchens. And I think the Crawfords would know if there *was* one hanging around their house. Maybe it was just a hose or a jump rope."

A stubborn expression appeared on Flash's face. "It *was* a snake! A huge one. And they won't know about it because it's hiding behind the refrigerator! I saw it slither over there when Mom came into the kitchen."

Joe scratched his head. "But how could a

snake just sneak into someone's house without them seeing it?"

"I don't know!" Flash said firmly. "But you've got to stop it before it gobbles up my friends!"

CHAPTER THREE

Joe wasn't sure what to do next. He wanted to help Flash, but he couldn't exactly call the Crawfords and tell them there was a snake hiding in their kitchen. They'd never believe him. He still wasn't sure he believed it himself!

"Come on," he said. "Maybe we can find out what kind of snake you *think* you saw."

"Hey!" squealed the guinea pig as Joe picked him up and squashed him into the large front pocket of his hoodie.

Joe crept out into the hall and listened. He

could hear Toby splashing around in the bath upstairs. Dad was talking to him. He could hear Mom up there, too, moving around. Luckily, he didn't have to worry about Sarah—his pain-in-the-neck big sister was at sleepaway camp.

Joe snuck into the kitchen and spotted Dad's new tablet computer lying on the table. He lifted Flash out of his pocket, then switched on the tablet and typed in the word *snake*.

"What color was it?" asked Joe.

"Orange!"

"And how big was it?"

"Enormous!" Flash gasped.

Joe smiled. "Yeah, but everything looks enormous to you, Flash, because you're so little!"

Flash made an indignant snorting noise, and a stream of bubbles burst out of his nose. "It was nearly as long as this table!"

"Really?" Joe figured the kitchen table was

about three feet wide. If there really *was* a snake, it was a big one! He tapped in the details.

Joe found a site about exotic pets in the search results. He opened the page and then clicked on a photo of an orange snake. "There!" He pointed. "Is that it?"

Flash looked at the picture of the snake and gave a squeal. "That's it!"

Joe read the text. "It's a corn snake," he said. "It says they're not dangerous to people . . ."

"But what about guinea pigs?"

Joe read some more. "Oh."

"What? What is it, Joe?"

"It says corn snakes should be kept away from other pets . . . and . . ."

"What?" Flash looked up at Joe. "Tell me!"

"Well, it says that a corn snake's main source of food is . . . small rodents!"

Flash gave a superloud squeak, and a rush of bubbles popped out of his ears, filling the

UNDEAD PETS

air with a flowery scent.

"Joe?"

Mom was standing in the doorway. "What are you doing? And what's that smell? Have you been spraying air freshener?"

"No!" Joe shook his head. "It's nothing to do with me!"

Mom rubbed her nose. She couldn't see the undead pets—no one could, except Joe. But thanks to her allergies she could always sense when one was close.

"Why are you using Dad's tablet?" Mom asked. "You know he said you had to get permission."

Joe felt his face turn red. "I was just finding out about . . . animals."

Mom sighed. "I know how much you love animals, and I could see that you and Toby had a great time playing with the guinea pigs, but we've been through this hundreds of times! We can't get a pet because of my allergies."

"But you didn't sneeze so much today, Mom. Maybe guinea pigs don't bother you like other animals do."

"No, it's because I took an allergy pill. But the medicine doesn't make my allergies disappear altogether. In fact"—she wrinkled her nose and blinked a few times—"it must be wearing off. My nose actually feels a bit tickly now . . ." She rubbed her eyes. "Turn off the tablet now, please, Joe." She turned and left the room.

Joe waited until she'd gone then looked back at the screen. "I just want to check one more thing..." He tapped in the words *escaped snake*, then hit ENTER.

"Wow!" he gasped. There were hundreds of stories about people finding escaped snakes in their houses. Maybe Flash's story wasn't as crazy as he'd thought! Joe clicked on one story, and a picture of a giant python lying on a bathroom radiator appeared.

Joe could hear his mom calling him again. He scooped up Flash and headed for the door.

"What are we going to do now?" Flash squeaked.

"I'm sure I'll think of something," whispered Joe, climbing into bed later that night. "Maybe I could go over to the Crawfords' house tomorrow morning to try to find the snake..."

Flash sighed. "If it's not already too late."

Joe placed Flash in an old shoe box stuffed

with socks then lay down and flicked his bedside light off.

A moment later he felt something cold and soggy wriggling by his feet. The next second, Flash popped his head out from under the duvet onto Joe's pillow.

"Guinea pigs stick together," squeaked Flash, nuzzling up to Joe.

"But I'm not a guinea pig!" Joe grimaced. "Move over!" he added, annoyed. But Flash was already asleep, snoring bubbles.

CHAPTER FOUR

The next morning, Toby was standing in his pajamas, watching Joe put on his sneakers.

"Where are you going?" Toby asked.

"Out!" said Joe. He was trying not to squish Flash as he leaned over. The guinea pig was tucked inside his hoodie pocket again. "On my bike!"

"Why?"

"Because I want to."

"But we're going bowling today," said Toby, who had slipped on Dad's shoes and was clomping around in the hallway next to Joe.

Joe groaned. He'd forgotten that he was supposed to be meeting his friends Matt and Ben at the bowling alley.

Joe glanced at the clock. "That's not until eleven o'clock, right? I'm going out on my bike first. See you!"

Joe slipped out of the front door before Dad appeared.

"I hope we're not too late," squeaked Flash, popping out his pink nose and sniffing the morning air. "The snake might have got them already!"

"I doubt it," muttered Joe, "or I'd have had two more undead pets in my bed this morning!" He grabbed his bike from the side of the house and climbed on. "I hope the Crawfords let me in."

The plan was to bike over to the Crawfords' house and pretend he'd left his hat there.

UNDEAD PETS

I wonder if they'll remember I wasn't actually wearing a hat yesterday, Joe thought.

As they hurtled down the road, Flash let out an excited squeal. "Faster, Joe!"

Less than five minutes later, they were outside the Crawfords' house. Joe took a deep breath and pressed the doorbell. He shuffled his feet impatiently, his confidence disappearing.

Flash wriggled out of Joe's pocket. "I'll sneak inside and take a look."

He scrambled down Joe's leg and disappeared straight through the front door.

Joe rang the bell again.

"They're out, loser!"

Joe spun around to find Spiker—the most annoying boy in his class—smirking at him from the yard next door.

"What are you doing here?" Joe spluttered.

"I live here!"

UNDEAD PETS

"What?"

Spiker rolled his eyes and nodded at the house next door to the Crawfords'.

"That's mine, dummy!" Then his eyes narrowed. "What are *you* doing here?"

Before Joe could answer, a smug smile appeared on Spiker's face. "Are you Erin's boyfriend?"

"No!"

UNDEAD PETS

"Joe loves Erin!" Spiker sang.

Joe felt his face turn beet red. "Get lost!"

"Wait till I tell everyone at school!"

"No!"

Just then, Flash reappeared through the wall of the Crawfords' house. "They're out, Joe. I saw a window open at the back of the house. Sneak inside so you can hunt for the snake!"

Joe frowned. Even if Spiker hadn't been

there, there was no way he was going to break into someone's house!

"Talk to me, Joe!" squealed Flash. "What's the plan?" He scrabbled anxiously at Joe's ankles, scratching him through his socks. "Do something!"

Joe gave Flash an exasperated look. Didn't he understand they were being watched? He bent down and pretended to retie his shoelace. "We'll come back later!" he hissed.

"Want me to tell Erin you stopped by?" shouted Spiker.

"What?"

"I'll tell her you send your LOVE!" Spiker made a sappy face.

"GET LOST!" Joe scooped up Flash, stuffed him back in his pocket, and headed for his bike.

"No!" Angry bubbles exploded from Flash's nose. "What about my friends? Guinea pigs stick together!"

Joe didn't answer. As he got on his bike, he expected Spiker to tease him again. But he didn't. Spiker's back was turned, and he appeared to be looking for something in the bushes.

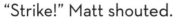

"Strike!" Matt shouted.

"Wow! You're on fire! High five!" Ben leaped up to slap palms with Matt.

The bowling alley was packed full of families enjoying the winter break.

Joe heard another yelp of delight from the lane next to them and watched Toby and his friend Ricky high-fiving, too.

"Even my little brother's doing better than me," Joe muttered.

Flash was scuttling around Joe's feet nonstop. "When can we go, Joe?" he was squeaking. "I'm worried—so worried."

UNDEAD PETS

The more Joe thought about the snake, the more anxious he felt. He could just picture the snake slithering across the kitchen, inching toward the guinea pigs . . .

"Strike!" yelled Ben, punching the air.

"Awesome!" Matt slapped Ben on the back. "But I'm still beating you."

"Just barely!" Ben replied.

Both boys looked at Joe. It was his turn next.

Joe ran his hands over all the bowling balls

and grasped a big purple one. It was really too big for him, but it looked impressive!

Joe staggered to the lane.

"Want me to get a strike for you, Joe?" Ben teased.

Joe shot him a glare then lunged forward, aiming as straight as he could. The weight of the ball made him lurch sideways, and he dropped it onto the lane heavily.

The ball began rolling slowly toward the pins.

Matt snorted, and Ben stifled a giggle.

Eventually the ball drifted left and dropped into the gutter.

"Tough break, Joe!" called Dad from the next lane. "Try a lighter ball!"

"Maybe you need the rubber bumpers, too." Matt chuckled. "Like the little kids have!"

Joe scowled.

"Sorry, buddy," Matt said. "Just kidding."

Joe grabbed another ball and stepped back onto the lane to bowl it. As he let go, Flash shot out from between his feet and zoomed down the lane in front of the ball.

"That looks better!" called Dad.

Joe's ball was much straighter this time, but it still lacked power—it certainly wasn't going fast enough to knock down all the pins.

BANG!

The ball slapped into the front pin. Three pins fell and a couple of others wobbled . . .

"Nah—you're not gonna get them all," said Matt. "Shame."

"Wait!" said Ben. "Look!"

More pins were falling.

Flash was streaking in and out, head-butting the pins. In seconds they were all down.

Ben and Matt stared.

"How did you do that?" Matt asked with a frown. Then he grinned. "High five!"

CHAPTER FIVE

"You were awesome, Joe!" said Toby as they got into the car to go home. "You smashed Matt and Ben!"

Flash gave a happy squeak. "Guinea pigs stick together!"

Joe grinned. For once he didn't mind being counted as a guinea pig. Thanks to Flash, Joe had won that game—and the one after. He'd even beaten his dad's score! Being Protector of Undead Pets had gotten Joe into a lot of tricky situations, so it was nice for one of the pets to actually do something to help him!

"Can we go for pizza?" Toby begged.

"Not today," said Dad. "But we need to do some shopping on the way home. Mom wants us to pick up something for George's birthday. Any ideas?"

"Guinea pigs!" shouted Toby.

"What?" Joe jumped. Could Toby see Flash?

"Let's get George something for his guinea pigs—some toys or something . . ."

Phew! Joe thought.

"Good idea!" said Dad. "We'll go to the pet store and have a look."

They pulled into a parking space.

"Don't worry," Joe whispered to Flash, putting the guinea pig back into his hoodie pocket. "It won't take long."

They got out of the car and Joe hung back behind Dad and Toby, pretending to fool around with his watch. "Maybe the store will have a book about snakes," Joe whispered. "We might get some ideas for where to look for it."

"The snake's behind the fridge!" snapped Flash. "I told you!"

"Yeah, but it might not have stayed in the same place. If it did, I think the Crawfords would have spotted it by now."

Joe ran to catch up with Toby and Dad.

The pet store was enormous.

UNDEAD PETS

"Joe!" called Toby. "Come and look at the guinea pigs!"

Flash let out an excited squeal. "Let me see, let me see!"

He scrambled down Joe's leg and hurtled after Toby, squeaking loudly.

Inside the pen was a gang of baby guinea pigs, munching hay. By the time Joe arrived, Flash was already in there, sniffing and nuzzling and making happy squeaky noises.

"Some of them are hiding!" said Toby,

pointing to a pair of smaller guinea pigs that were peeking out from inside a plastic pet house.

"They must be scared." Dad chuckled. "I would be, too, with your ugly mug staring at me!" He ruffled Toby's hair.

"Can we have one, Dad? Please!"

"Don't be silly, Toby. Come and choose some toys for George . . ."

Toby's shoulders slumped. Then he spotted another pen. "Wow! Rabbits!" he said, and raced over.

Joe lingered, looking at the guinea pigs. They were chasing one another around the pen now, with Flash joining in as though he was still alive.

Then Joe noticed a series of large tanks, right at the back of the store. He went over to take a closer look.

Two small geckos stared back at him out of

the first tank, their tiny ink-spot eyes following his every movement. Joe went over to the next tank, where a bright green chameleon sat on a log. The last tank was empty.

Joe was just about to go back to the chameleon when he felt a tap on his shoulder.

"Didn't see her, did you?" A young sales assistant was standing there with cleaning spray in one hand and a bucket of soapy water in the other. She smiled at Joe. "She's good at hiding."

Joe looked into the last tank again. Finally he spotted a small striped orange snake right at the back, half hidden under a curved piece of bark. It poked its tongue out at him. It was similar to the one he'd seen on the Internet only much smaller—it looked like a shoelace.

"Is it a corn snake?" asked Joe.

"Yep. It's just a baby. She'll grow much, much bigger."

UNDEAD PETS

Joe glanced over his shoulder to make sure Dad and Toby weren't listening. "Do pet snakes ever escape?" he asked.

"Oh yeah! Lucky, my boa constrictor, got out once. We tried all the tricks—laying out food, dusting the floors with flour to see if we could spot where she'd been . . . Then Mom found her at the back of the linen closet, snuggling into the warm towels!"

Joe grinned. He could just imagine what would happen if his mom found a snake in their closet! "Where else do they hide?" he asked.

"Anywhere warm. Snakes hate the cold. Sometimes they hide behind the refrigerator—the motor makes it hot there."

So that was why Flash saw the snake sneak behind the fridge! thought Joe.

"Down the back of the sofa," the girl went on, "under floorboards . . . Bigger snakes are quite strong. If you don't put a brick on top of the tank lid, they can push their way out! Are you thinking of getting one?"

Before Joe could answer there was a shout from the other side of the store. "Caitlin!" It was the pet-store owner, calling from the register. "Can you fetch a box of pinkies for this boy?"

Joe glanced over and gasped.

It was Spiker!

He hadn't noticed Joe yet. He was too busy counting out a pile of change.

"Gotta go!" the girl said, and she disappeared into a backroom.

Joe headed over to Dad and Toby, who were comparing guinea-pig toys. But as he passed the cash register he heard Spiker talking to the pet-store owner.

"And you think if I put out more snake food he'll come back?" Spiker asked.

Joe froze. Did he really just say "snake food"?

The man nodded. "Yep, if he's been missing for a few days, he's bound to get hungry soon. Just put some of his usual food—a couple of dead mice—near his tank. You can try other places, too. Corn snakes usually come back when they smell grub!"

Joe gasped. Spiker had lost a corn snake . . . and he lived next door to the Crawfords! That meant it was probably *his* snake that Flash had seen.

"What are you staring at?" Spiker growled, peering at Joe.

UNDEAD PETS

Joe shrugged. Then he had an idea. If he could somehow tempt the snake out of the Crawfords' house and back to Spiker's then all his troubles would be over!

"Did you say you've lost a snake?" asked Joe.

"No!" Spiker glanced around nervously. "You heard wrong."

"Here you go!" said Caitlin, arriving with a cardboard box. "Remember to defrost them before you feed them to your snake, okay?"

Spiker's face flushed, and he glared at Joe.

"Five dollars, please," said the pet-store owner.

Spiker was in such a rush to pay, he dropped the money on the floor. He bent down and scooped it up then counted everything out. But one coin was missing—he was twenty-five cents short.

"It must have gone under the counter," he mumbled.

"Here." Joe dug in his pocket and handed over a quarter.

"Thanks," Spiker muttered. Then he snatched up the box and turned to go.

"Wait!" said Joe. "My cousin lost his pet corn snake once . . ." He hoped the fib wouldn't show on his face. "I found it for him!"

"What? How?"

Joe shrugged. "You've just got to look in the right places."

"I've tried that—" Spiker stopped abruptly

when he realized he'd just admitted that he *had* lost a snake.

"I know lots of secret places that snakes like to hide in," said Joe. "And there's always the flour trick!"

"The what?"

Before Joe could explain, a woman appeared in the store.

"Bradley, there you are!" It was Mrs. Piker—Spiker's mom. Joe giggled—no one at school ever called Spiker by his real name. "We've only got a few minutes left on the parking meter—come on!" She glanced at Joe and immediately recognized him from Spiker's class. "Joe, isn't it?" She smiled. "Enjoying your break?"

"Yes, thanks."

"Great. Well, we've got to go now. Come on, Bradley!"

"Can Joe come over to our house?" Spiker said suddenly.

UNDEAD PETS

"What?" Joe turned to look at Spiker.

Mrs. Piker looked shocked, too. "Well, I—I . . . ," she stuttered.

"Joe wants to see Harley's pets," Spiker said. "And since I'm looking after them while he's away, maybe I could show Joe today."

Joe remembered now that Spiker had once done a school presentation about his brother's collection of exotic pets.

"Joe's thinking about getting a corn snake!" Spiker added. "Aren't you, Joe?"

"Um, yeah." Joe nodded, uncertainly.

"And he'd like to meet Thor!"

Joe wondered why Spiker didn't just say that he wanted Joe to come over and help look for his brother's lost snake . . . But then it hit Joe like a bolt of lightning. Mrs. Piker didn't know the snake had escaped!

"You boys and your snakes." She sighed, shaking her head. "Why you can't just have a nice hamster or a rabbit, I'll never know!"

"Can he come?" Spiker asked. "This afternoon?"

"I guess so," Mrs. Piker replied. "You'd better ask your dad, Joe. Is that him over there?"

CHAPTER SIX

"Weird!" said Toby as they pulled up outside Spiker's house a few hours later. "Why are you going to Spiker's house? You hate him!"

"I don't!" Joe felt his cheeks redden.

"It *is* a bit odd," added Dad. "I mean, you've never wanted to hang out with him before."

Flash, who was sitting on Joe's knee, gave a sudden squeak. "They're home!" He was looking at the Crawfords' car, which was now parked in the driveway outside their house. "I want to see Bolt and Lightning!"

UNDEAD PETS

As Joe opened the car door, Flash jumped off his knee, scrambled out, and raced up the Crawfords' path, disappearing into the house.

"Can we go and see George?" asked Toby, undoing his seatbelt.

"No!" said Dad firmly. "You'll see George tomorrow at the party."

Toby refastened his belt. "Okay."

Joe climbed out of the car and spotted Spiker waiting for him on his doorstep. Joe gulped. He felt like he was about to enter a dragon's lair.

"All right," mumbled Spiker. "Want to come upstairs?"

Spiker's house wasn't what Joe was expecting. In fact, it was just like Joe's.

"That's my room," Spiker said, nodding to the first door at the top of the stairs. "Go in, if you want."

It was bigger than Joe's bedroom and much

tidier. There were posters of snakes, lizards, and spiders on the walls. In the corner was a small TV with a beanbag chair next to it and a pile of games stacked nearby. Joe also noticed several wooden models on top of Spiker's dresser.

"Is that a lizard?" he asked, picking up the largest one.

"It's a Komodo dragon," said Spiker. "I made it with my grandpa. He's got an amazing workshop with lots of power tools."

Joe turned the model around to get a closer look.

"Careful! I spent a long time on that." Spiker took it from Joe and put it back on top of the dresser.

"Is that a rattlesnake?" Joe pointed to a poster above Spiker's bed.

"Yeah, it's an eastern diamondback rattlesnake. That's the largest poisonous snake in America!"

"I've got a tree python's tooth at home," Joe said.

"Yeah, right!" Spiker rolled his eyes.

"No, really! My great-uncle Charlie got bitten by one when he was trekking through the rain forest in Australia! He brought the tooth back as a present for me."

Spiker shook his head. "I don't believe you."

"It's true—you can stop by and see it if you want."

"Yeah?"

Joe nodded. Then he realized that he'd just invited his least favorite boy in the whole school over to his house. Working together to catch the snake was one thing, but hanging out together was another matter!

"Cool! A tarantula!" Joe said, pointing at another poster to change the subject.

"Yeah! Harley's got a real one. Do you want to see it?"

Joe followed Spiker back into the hall.

"We've got to wash our hands first," Spiker said.

"What?" Joe asked, frowning.

"The bathroom's here. We shouldn't bring germs into the room," Spiker explained.

Joe looked at Spiker to figure out whether he was joking, but he was deadly serious.

They both washed their hands, and then Spiker led the way to Harley's room.

It was a bit like a jungle. The curtains were almost closed, and the tank lights gave the room a greenish-yellow glow.

"Don't touch anything," hissed Spiker. "Harley's got it all set at the right temperature. These creatures are very delicate!" Spiker crouched down by a plastic tank that contained an enormous hairy tarantula. "This is Zena," he said. "She's awesome, isn't she! Want to hold her?"

Joe hesitated. He didn't want Spiker to think he was a wimp, but didn't tarantulas bite?

"Ha! Just kidding!" Spiker smirked.

Joe tried not to look too relieved. "Does she bite?"

"Nah . . ."

Joe looked at the other tanks. In one, a small spotted lizard was staring out at them.

"That's a leopard gecko," Spiker told Joe. "There are two of them in there, but the other one's shy. And that's Cheese next door..."

"Cheese?" Joe looked into the next tank.

"Yeah, his friend's called Pickle."

Joe smiled. "Is he a turtle?"

"No, he's a terrapin. Want to hold him?"

This time he wasn't joking.

"Remember, be careful!" growled Spiker. "Look, I'll show you..." He picked the terrapin up out of the tank. "You support him under his body like this."

He handed the terrapin to Joe, watching him like a hawk. "If you drop him, he'll die." Spiker glared menacingly at Joe. "And so will you!"

"He's amazing!" said Joe, peering at the tiny creature in his hand. "How do you know so much about all these animals?"

Spiker put the terrapin back in the tank. "Harley works at the Reptile Rescue Group in town. They re-home reptiles and amphibians."

UNDEAD PETS

"What do you mean?" Joe asked.

Spiker shook his head. "They save abandoned pets! Some people don't want them when they get bigger. Or they don't look after them the right way. So Reptile Rescue finds them new homes. Most of Harley's creatures come from there. He's just taking care of them till they find permanent homes."

Joe looked around. It was strange to think these cool creatures were all unwanted pets.

"I'm gonna help the rescue group, too, when I'm old enough," Spiker said proudly.

"So what happened to Thor?" Joe asked.

Spiker looked embarrassed. "Harley's away for a few days on a training course. Me and Dad are looking after the animals for him. It's pretty easy. I can manage most of it myself. But I'm not allowed to touch the snakes without Dad."

"Then how did Thor escape?"

Spiker shrugged. "Thor's my favorite. I

only had him out for five minutes. I must have forgotten to put the brick on the lid of his tank when I put him back."

"And he pushed his way out?" asked Joe.

"Don't tell my parents! They'll never let me get a snake of my own if they find out!"

"Haven't they noticed?"

"No. Mom doesn't like the reptiles, so she never comes in here, and Dad trusts me. The snakes don't need to be fed every day . . ."

Joe nodded. He remembered reading that on the Internet.

"Most of the time Dad just pops in and checks the sheet." Spiker pointed to a clipboard lying on the bed. "Harley makes me tick a feeding and care sheet for them all." Spiker frowned. "Anyway, we're gonna find Thor, aren't we? We've got to," he growled, "or Harley will kill me!"

CHAPTER SEVEN

"Joe, Joe!"

Flash had appeared in Harley's bedroom. "You've got to come and look for the snake. I can smell it, but I can't see it!"

Suddenly Flash froze. He glanced around at all the strange creatures in the room then threw himself at Joe's feet, shaking like jelly. "What is this place? It's horrible!" Perfumed bubbles exploded out of Flash's nose.

Spiker sniffed the air and looked at Joe suspiciously.

Joe coughed. "Should we start searching for Thor now?" he said to Spiker. "I bet there are lots of places a snake could hide in here."

Flash gave an indignant snort. "The snake's not in here!" He head-butted Joe's ankle angrily. "The snake's next door!"

"Let's wash our hands again—then we'll start looking," said Spiker.

"What?" Joe frowned. "But we just washed them!"

"But we touched the terrapin. They can spread salmonella," Spiker replied.

Spiker is never this sensible at school! Joe thought.

"You go first," said Spiker. "I've got to check the terrapins' tank to make sure the lid is on tight."

Flash followed Joe into the bathroom. "You've got to come and find that snake! Now!"

Joe turned on the tap then scooped up

Flash. "Listen, Flash," he whispered. "Thor might have come back here again—he could be in Spiker's house now. We're going to look for him!"

"The snake is *not* here," Flash snorted. "It's next door!"

"Well, maybe I can find out how he got next door and then put some food down to tempt him back. That's what the man at the pet store told Spiker to do. It's worth a try!"

For the next hour they looked everywhere. Luckily Spiker's mom was too busy gardening to notice.

"Check the trash can!" said Joe as they looked inside the kitchen cabinets. "And behind the refrigerator. The motor makes it warm back there."

"It's not there!" grumbled Flash from Joe's pocket. "I've told you—the snake's next door!"

"Where did you find your cousin's snake?" asked Spiker.

Joe blushed. He hated fibbing. "It was inside the linen closet," he said, remembering where the girl in the store had found her boa constrictor.

"Okay—we'll look there, too!"

Ten minutes later they were back upstairs in Harley's room.

"Nothing," groaned Spiker. "Harley's going to go ballistic!"

Joe didn't reply. He was on his hands and knees, peering behind Thor's tank. He could see a large crack in the radiator. He stood up and patted the wall. "This leads through to next door, doesn't it?"

Spiker nodded.

"What if Thor crawled through the gap

behind the tank? Maybe he got through to the house next door."

"Ha!" scoffed Spiker. "I think I'd have heard if a snake had appeared in the Crawfords' house!"

"It has, it has!" squealed Flash.

"Yeah," said Joe, "but what if he's found somewhere cozy to hide? Maybe they don't know."

"Mom would go crazy!" Spiker replied.

"Go get some snake food and leave it by this crack," said Joe. "Maybe the smell will make Thor come back. When did you last feed him?"

"A few days ago. So he'll be getting hungry," said Spiker. "I'll go get some dead mice to put out for him."

"Dead mice!" squeaked Flash. Joe's pocket began to quake.

"AHHHHH!" Joe sat bolt upright in the darkness.

"What is it, Joe?" Flash poked his head out from under the covers.

"SNAKES!" Joe gasped. "EVERYWHERE!"

Flash gave a squeal and dived back under the covers.

"Joe?" His bedroom light went on. Dad stood in the doorway.

Joe blinked a few times, then realized he'd just been dreaming.

After spending the afternoon at Spiker's house, all he'd been able to think about was snakes! Now he was dreaming about them, too.

"Snakes," Joe said, suddenly feeling a bit silly. "They were everywhere! Under the floorboards, slithering out of the faucets, in the toilet . . ."

"I think you've been spending too much time with Spiker and his scary pets!" said Dad.

"They're not scary—they're amazing, really . . ."

"I'll take your word for it, Joe! Good night!" Dad turned off the light and shut the door.

"You can come out now!" whispered Joe.

Flash gave a squeak. "Not until the snakes have gone!"

"There weren't any snakes. I was just dreaming."

Flash scrabbled up. "Are you sure? Poor Bolt and Lightning—I wonder if they've seen the snake. They'll be terrified! And what if it's already eaten them?" grumbled Flash.

"Thor's probably back in Harley's room by now," said Joe. "You'll be gone by the morning!"

"What?"

"Well," mumbled Joe sleepily, "if Thor goes home, your problems will be solved." *And I'll get my bed back to myself*, he thought with a smile.

But when morning came, Flash was still there.

UNDEAD PETS

"I don't want to go to the dentist today!" wailed Toby, who was sitting at the kitchen table, squishing the last bits of his cereal with the back of his spoon. "Why do we have to go? We're on vacation!"

Mom ignored him. "Hurry up with your breakfast, Joe," she said, picking up Toby's bowl and putting it in the sink. "And, Toby, go and brush your teeth." Then she turned to

Dad. "Don't forget you're dropping Toby off at George's party this afternoon—I've got clients until five o'clock. Are you sure you don't want to go, Joe?"

"What?" Joe was thinking about snakes again.

"The party—at George and Erin's house?"

Joe frowned. Maybe he *should* go. To see if he could spot the snake . . .

"Don't you want to see Doctor Franken-Bubble?" asked Toby, prodding Joe's arm. "The monster party's going to be so exciting!"

Yeah, thought Joe, *especially if an enormous snake shows up!*

CHAPTER EIGHT

The dentist's waiting room was large and airy with huge squishy sofas. Joe recognized a few kids from school waiting with their parents. Toby and a girl from his class were checking out a cabinet full of toothbrushes.

"I want that one!" Toby said, pointing to a green brush with a monster's head on the end. "Or the troll one. It's really cool!"

"Maybe later," Mom said, wiping her nose with a tissue. Her allergies were bothering her again, thanks to Flash's fur. She blew her nose noisily. "We're up next!"

At that moment the dental hygienist appeared. "Joe and Toby Edmunds? Follow me."

Joe slipped off his coat with Flash still inside the pocket. "Wait here!" he whispered, laying it on the back of the sofa next to Toby's fleece.

Flash gave an impatient snort.

The nurse led them into the exam room.

"Who's going first?" asked Dr. Ridge, the dentist.

"Joe!" squeaked Toby, who'd spotted the dentist's shiny instruments lined up on a stand next to the big black chair. "Can I go to the bathroom?"

Mom sighed. "Can't you wait?"

Toby made a face. "I'm desperate!"

"Come on then." Mom took his hand. "I'll show you where it is."

Joe climbed into the chair.

"If you could just put these glasses on, then sit back," said the nurse.

Joe blinked under the bright lights.

"Open wide," said Dr. Ridge.

As he began working on Joe's teeth, tapping, prodding, and checking each one in turn, Joe heard a noise by the door. It was the sound of scratchy small footsteps.

"Joe?" squeaked Flash. "JOE! What's that man doing to you? Is he the vet?"

Joe groaned. He was helpless—he couldn't move, he couldn't speak, there was no way he could tell Flash what was happening. He wriggled anxiously.

Dr. Ridge stopped for a moment. "Everything okay, Joe? Does it hurt there?"

Joe shook his head.

"What's he doing?" squeaked Flash.

Joe gripped the chair with frustration. Why hadn't Flash stayed in the waiting room?

UNDEAD PETS

"Is he hurting you?" Flash squealed.

Joe turned his head slightly, trying to catch a glimpse of Flash and show him he was fine.

"It's okay, Joe," the dentist said soothingly. "We're almost finished. Nothing to worry about . . ."

"Joe? Joe? Speak to me!" Flash was jumping up and down, flowery bubbles erupting from his nose.

At that moment, Mom and Toby came back in. Mom let out a sudden sneeze!

Joe jumped and Dr. Ridge stepped back, bumping into the stand holding his equipment.

It wobbled and then . . .

"Look out!" called the nurse, as the instruments clattered down to the floor.

"Oops!" Toby giggled. "Does that mean I miss my turn?"

"I'm so, so sorry," Mom kept saying as she made their next appointment.

The receptionist smiled patiently. "It wasn't your fault, Mrs. Edmunds."

Mom blew her nose. "My allergies have been terrible lately!"

Joe felt his face turn red. He shoved Flash even deeper into his coat pocket.

"Hey!" the guinea pig squeaked. "I can't breathe!"

You don't need to! thought Joe. *You're already dead!*

"Look!" Toby nudged Joe. "It's Spiker!"

Joe glanced up. It was Spiker.

AACHOOO!

"What's up, Joe?" Spiker said.

"What are you doing here?" Joe asked.

"Same as you!" Spiker grinned.

"I'll just tell them we're here," Mrs. Piker said. "Hello again, Joe. We seem to be seeing a lot of you lately!" She smiled and headed to the reception desk.

Toby had spotted the toothbrushes again. "Mom! Can I have the troll one?"

"Any sign of Thor?" Joe whispered to Spiker.

Spiker glanced over at Toby. "Nah," he muttered.

"There's still time," Joe said hopefully.

Spiker nodded. "He'll be starving by now!"

"What?" Flash poked his head out of Joe's pocket. "Did you hear that?" he squeaked. "The snake's starving, and I know what he'll want for dinner—fresh guinea pig, that's what!"

UNDEAD PETS

"I'm going to a party today," said Toby, coming over to Joe and Spiker.

"Great!" said Spiker.

"There's going to be lots of awesome food. Pizza, hamburgers, hot dogs . . . I love hot dogs!"

Joe was just about to tell Toby to put a sock in it when a horrible thought wriggled into his brain. What if Thor was attracted to the party food instead of his snake grub? Did snakes eat hot dogs?

"It's at George's house," Toby went on. "Next door to you! And there's going to be lots of kids and games and prizes. And Doctor Franken-Bubble!"

"What?" Spiker was listening now. "George is having a party? A big one?"

Toby nodded. "Do you want to go?"

"No, thanks!" Spiker said. Then he turned to Joe and dropped his voice to a whisper, so only Joe could hear. "If Thor is in the Crawfords' house, he'll be terrified of the noise. Snakes get stressed!"

"What?" Joe looked at Spiker.

"Snakes are sensitive creatures!" Spiker hissed.

"Ha!" Flash snorted. "Sensitive creatures? As if! More like slithery, guinea-pig gobbling slimeballs!"

"And we're gonna play hot potato and have a treasure hunt," Toby added.

Spiker's eyes narrowed. "Little kids are terrible around snakes." He scowled at Toby.

"They're too rough and noisy!"

Joe hadn't really thought about the snake's feelings before. After all, it was a pet, too. "We've got to find Thor!" he said quietly.

"How?" Spiker demanded.

"I'll go to the party," said Joe.

"Oh, how terrible . . ."

Mom was on the phone with Mrs. Crawford. She was asking if it would be all right for Joe to go to the party. When he'd told her he'd changed his mind, she'd nearly crashed the car! He'd told her that he decided he wanted to see the bubble man.

"Oh, yes," Mom was saying to Mrs. Crawford. "I can imagine Erin and George must have been devastated."

"What is it?" Toby looked at Joe across the lunch table.

Joe shrugged.

"Yes," Mom went on. "He was so cute. That adorable squeaking noise he made . . . It's so sad you've lost him."

Joe gulped. It sounded like another guinea pig had died!

"Oh dear," Mom added, nodding. She was quiet for a while, then after a few moments, she said, "Thanks so much, the boys can't wait!"

Mom ended the phone call and looked at Joe and Toby with a glum expression on her face. "I'm really sorry, boys, but I'm afraid I've got some sad news."

"What?" Toby looked terrified. "The party's not canceled, is it?"

"No, Carol's looking forward to seeing you both this afternoon. But I'm afraid one of Erin and George's guinea pigs has died."

"NO!" squealed Flash, who was snuffling around under the table next to Joe's feet. "The snake must have gotten them!"

Joe felt his throat go tight. He'd failed in his mission. One of the guinea pigs had been gobbled up!

"Which one?" asked Toby, his voice a bit quivery.

"Flash!" said Mom. "I'm really sorry."

"Who? What? Me?" From under the table, Flash gave a shocked squeak.

Of course! Joe sighed with relief. Mrs. Crawford was telling Mom about Flash's tragic end in the washing machine. Joe had forgotten that no one else knew what had happened to Flash after they'd left the Crawfords' house.

He tried not to smile. If only Mom and Toby knew that, at that very moment, Flash was sitting on the floor nibbling Toby's lunch crumbs!

"That's so sad," said Toby. His lip was trembling. "I liked Flash best!"

Flash puffed up his chest proudly.

"What are you going to wear to the party, Joe?" asked Mom, trying to change the subject.

"It's a monster party," said Toby, still looking tearful. "I'm going as a troll."

Joe looked desperately at Mom. "I don't have to dress up, do I?"

Mom smiled and shook her head. "Don't worry, Joe. You can wear whatever you want!"

CHAPTER NINE

A few hours later, Dad, Joe, and Toby were on the Crawfords' doorstep. There were balloons tied to the mailbox and a big HAPPY BIRTHDAY banner taped across the front door. Flash had already scrambled out of Joe's backpack and vanished into the house.

Through the front window they could see a crowd of kids dancing around the living room. The sound of laughter and shrieking and loud music boomed out.

"Do you think the present will be okay?"

asked Dad, ringing the bell again. "Maybe guinea-pig toys aren't the best thing to give a boy whose pet has just died!"

Toby hugged the brightly wrapped box tightly. "He's still got Bolt and Lightning!"

Not for much longer if I don't find that snake, thought Joe.

"Toby! Joe!" The door burst open and George stood there, wearing a Frankenstein costume. He had pretend bolts, through his neck and scars painted on his face. "We're playing musical statues!"

"Hi, Joe," said Erin, appearing behind Toby. She was dressed as a zombie—her hair messy, her raggedy dress covered in red paint. "Want to come to the kitchen—away from the little kids?"

"Hey!" George made a face, then darted off. "Quick, Toby!" he yelled. "In the living room."

"Good-bye then, boys! Have fun." Joe's dad turned and headed toward the car.

"Do you want some lemonade, Joe?" asked Erin. "Watch out!" she yelped as three small monsters zoomed past them, spilling handfuls of cheese puffs everywhere.

"Wow!" Joe said when he saw the kitchen.

Every surface was covered with food, and right in the middle was a giant chocolate monster cake!

"Help yourself to some snacks," Erin said.

As Joe scooped up a handful of chips, Erin poured some lemonade into two paper cups.

"I'm laying out the treasure-hunt clues. You can help me if you want."

"Uh-huh," mumbled Joe, but he wasn't listening. He was checking behind the refrigerator. Was Thor there?

"What are you doing?" Erin gave him a funny look.

"Nothing," said Joe. "I think we've got the same fridge as you . . . ," he added.

"Did your mom tell you what happened to Flash?"

Joe nodded.

"I miss him!" Erin sniffed.

Joe shuffled his feet uncomfortably. He never knew what to say when people were upset.

"JOE!" Flash burst into the room. "The guinea pigs are gone. They're not in their hutch!"

"Where are they?" Joe said, realizing too

late that he had spoken to Flash out loud.

"Who?" Erin frowned.

"Um, I mean, where are the other guinea pigs?" asked Joe.

"Outside in their run. Mom thought it would be safer for them with all the little kids in the house."

"Phew!" said Flash. "All right, let's start looking for the snake." He vanished back through the kitchen door.

"Where are you going to hide the clues?" Joe asked Erin, taking a quick look in the kitchen trash can, just in case Thor had snuck inside.

"I've already done most of them. There's just a few we need to put upstairs." Erin picked up some bits of paper and a role of Scotch tape and headed for the door. "Follow me!"

As soon as her back was turned, Joe quickly opened a couple of kitchen cabinets and glanced inside.

"Joe?" Erin was watching him.

"Sorry! I like your cabinets. They . . . don't creak when you open them." He wiggled them a bit. "See? Ours creak all the time!"

"Oh, right," said Erin, looking at him as though he was crazy. "Anyway, come on."

For the next ten minutes Joe helped Erin with the clues, keeping an eye out for the snake the whole time. He checked inside the laundry basket, in the closets, under the beds . . .

"Come on," Erin called from the bathroom.

Undead Pets

As Joe crossed the landing, Flash zoomed out through a door. "Seen it?" he squeaked.

Joe shook his head.

"Me neither. Hurry, Joe—this is our only chance!" And he scuttled off again, vanishing through another door.

Inside the bathroom, Joe noticed a tall cupboard with a latch at the top. At the bottom of it, next to the radiator, was a small hole. Joe studied it. Was it big enough for a snake to squeeze through? "What's in there?"

"That's the door to the attic," said Erin, taping the last clue to a shampoo bottle.

"Can I look inside?"

"No, Dad doesn't like us playing up there. It's not safe—there are no real floorboards."

Joe looked at the hole again and then up at the ceiling. What if that was the way Thor had gotten into the house? Maybe he'd wriggled over from Harley's bedroom into the

Crawfords' house? Maybe he was up there now!

Joe thought quickly. "Erin, I just need to use the bathroom."

After she'd left the bathroom, Joe stood on tiptoe and unhooked the latch on the door that led to the attic.

"Joe? What is it?" Flash had appeared through the bathroom door. "Have you found something?"

"I'm not sure . . ." Joe opened the door. Inside was a narrow cupboard with a ladder leading up to the attic. There was a flashlight on the ground.

"Pick me up, Joe!"

With Flash clinging to his shoulder and the flashlight tucked into his belt, Joe began climbing the ladder.

"Hey!" Joe yelped, halfway up. "Don't hold on so tight. It hurts!"

UNDEAD PETS

"I can't help it!" squeaked Flash. "I'm nervous. What if it's up there?"

"Well, it can't hurt you. You're dead already!" Joe replied.

But he was thinking the same thing. He'd never come eyeball to eyeball with a snake before. Even if Thor wasn't dangerous to humans, Joe still didn't like the idea of creeping up on him!

Cautiously, Joe eased his head up through the hole. He turned on the flashlight and shone it around.

"Nothing." He breathed a sigh of relief. "Just some spiders and a few bits of old junk!"

"Hey!" Joe felt a tug on his leg. He turned and bumped his head. "Ow!"

"What are you doing? I heard you banging around in there!" Erin was staring up at him. "Dad will go crazy if he sees you!"

Joe floundered, desperately trying to think of a cover story.

"Don't tell me. You want to know if our attic is as dusty as yours!" Erin said sarcastically.

Joe flicked the flashlight off and clambered down.

"Tell her, Joe. Erin will understand. She's nice," said Flash.

Joe hesitated, then he sighed and said, "I'm looking for a snake."

"What?" Erin rolled her eyes. "Very funny!"

"It's true! It escaped from Spiker's house—you know, the boy next door. It's a corn snake called Thor. Me and Spiker think it's come through the wall into your house."

"Awesome!" Erin breathed.

"Aren't you freaked out?"

Erin shook her head. "I love snakes!"

"How could she!" Flash squeaked indignantly.

"It's just that, I thought maybe you wouldn't want it near the guinea pigs . . ."

Erin's face fell. "Do snakes eat guinea pigs?"

"Well, they eat mice," said Joe.

"Oh!" Erin looked worried. "Where could it be?" She glanced around the bathroom.

"I've looked everywhere." Joe sighed. "I thought the attic was a good bet, but it's probably too cold up there. Snakes like the heat." Joe flicked some dust and cobwebs off his shirt. "I'm not sure where to look next."

Erin frowned. "I don't understand why we haven't seen it. Mom and Dad have been cleaning for days for George's party. How come they didn't spot it?"

Joe shrugged.

"Maybe it's gone home again," said Erin.

"We could check with Spiker," Joe suggested.

Just then there was a loud cheer from the

backyard, followed by excited shrieks.

Erin flipped open the bathroom window and looked out. "It's Doctor Franken-Bubble!"

Joe looked over her shoulder. A crazy-looking man with a green wig, a white lab coat, and bright red pants was standing in the middle of the lawn with a bubble blower. It was spitting out hundreds of bubbles.

"ERIN! JOE!"

"That's Mom," said Erin. "Come on, we'd better go down."

CHAPTER TEN

By the time Joe and Erin got outside, the lawn was a sea of bubbles. George and his friends were racing around after them.

"Look, Joe!" shouted Toby. "They're amazing!"

"I can see Lightning and Bolt!" squeaked Flash. "Put me down, Joe!"

The guinea pigs were on the other side of the yard in their run.

"I'm going to check on them," Flash said.

Joe looked around the yard. Maybe Thor

was out here somewhere, soaking up the sunshine!

Just then, there was a squeal of excitement from the children as Doctor Franken-Bubble picked up an enormous hoop, dipped it in a wading pool full of soapy bubble mixture, and waved it above his head, making the most humongous bubble Joe had ever seen!

"In a moment, I'll show you how to put a boy inside a bubble!" shouted Doctor Franken-

UNDEAD PETS

Bubble. "But first, let's turn up the bubble machine!"

Joe spotted Spiker waving to him from across the fence.

"Did you find Thor?" Spiker demanded.

Before Joe could answer, Erin appeared.

"We've looked everywhere," she said. "But there's no sign of your snake!"

Spiker glared at Joe. "Did you tell her?"

"It's okay. I like snakes." Erin smiled.

"Really?" Spiker's face softened a little. Then his frown returned. "We've got to find him! Harley's on his way home. He's just called Mom—he's coming back early. If Thor's not in his tank, I'll be dog food!"

"JOE! JOE!" Flash came hurtling over. "Joe! Stop them!" he squeaked. "They're taking the guinea pigs inside!"

Joe turned. Doctor Franken-Bubble was taking a break. He was chatting with Erin's mom and dad, with a mug of coffee in his hand, while the kids chased after bubbles from his automatic bubble machine.

But that wasn't what was upsetting Flash.

"Look!" he squealed.

A small group of children were disappearing back inside. George and Toby were among them—and they had Bolt and Lightning in their arms!

"What are they doing?" said Erin. "Mom

told George not to get the guinea pigs out when there are so many kids around. They'll be terrified!"

"The obstacle course," groaned Joe. "Toby was talking about it in the car. I bet he asked George to set it up again."

"The snake will get them!" squealed Flash.

"We'd better stop them." Erin turned to Spiker. "Want to come and look for the snake?"

Spiker nodded. He climbed over the fence. Joe scooped up Flash and shoved him into his pocket. They all raced across the lawn.

As they reached the house, Joe heard a shriek from inside. It sounded like Toby!

The kitchen was in chaos.

"They've escaped!" Toby was yelling.

George was crying.

"What happened?" Erin demanded. "Where are the guinea pigs?"

"They got scared and ran off!" he wailed.

UNDEAD PETS

"Found one!" shouted a girl from the kitchen. Erin went off to see.

"It's Lightning!" she called back a moment later. "No sign of Bolt, though."

George began crying even more.

"Stop it, you're making too much noise!" growled Spiker. "Snakes hate noise," he added in a whisper to Joe.

Joe glared at Spiker. His pet wasn't the only one in danger. What if the snake had gotten the guinea pig?

"I'm going to look for Thor," said Spiker, heading upstairs.

"What about Bolt?" squeaked Flash. "Find him, Joe!"

"Check the hall!" shouted Erin from the living room. "See if Bolt's in with the shoes."

Joe raced over to the shoe basket and began rummaging inside . . .

Nothing! He groaned. Then he spotted a gym bag by the front door. He pulled it open. *Someone's sweaty socks, but no guinea pig!*

"Any luck?" shouted Erin.

"Do something, Joe," squeaked Flash. "We have to save Bolt! He could be getting gobbled up right now!"

Joe looked around desperately. Where would a panicking guinea pig go? Suddenly, he had an idea. He leaned in close to Flash.

"Where would you hide in the house if you were scared?"

"What?" Flash stopped squeaking and looked at Joe.

"Where would you hide? That's where Bolt will be!"

Flash twitched his nose. "Under the floorboards in the dining room!"

"What?"

"There's a gap behind the bookcase. I went there once when I escaped out of my hutch," Flash squeaked.

Joe dashed into the dining room. He spotted the bookcase immediately.

"Bolt?" he called, bending down to look.

"See," said Flash. "There's a gap behind it."

Joe looked around and saw a half-broken floorboard, with a gap big enough for a guinea pig to hide in. He tugged at it and then gasped.

An orange snake's head popped out, its tongue flicking as it sniffed the air.

Flash gave a loud squeal and darted away.

UNDEAD PETS

"Thor!" Joe breathed.

"You found him!" Spiker appeared behind Joe. His face was glowing with happiness. He carefully picked up the snake. It wrapped its body around Spiker's arms. "You're safe now," he crooned.

"It's a good thing we found him," Joe said. "He might have gobbled up Bolt!"

Spiker rolled his eyes. "Thor prefers dead mice!"

"Wow!" Erin appeared next to them. "He's awesome!"

"Where's Bolt?" asked Joe.

"He was in the kitchen, hiding behind the vegetable rack. George's getting in trouble with Mom!" Erin giggled. She pointed to the snake. "Can I hold him?"

"He's a bit scared of strangers," said Spiker.

"WHAT'S GOING ON IN HERE?" Erin's mom stood in the doorway. She blinked at the snake as though she couldn't believe her eyes.

"This is Spiker from next door and his pet snake, Thor," said Erin calmly. "I asked Spiker to bring him over to show George, as a special treat for his birthday."

"That's very kind of you . . . Spiker," Mrs. Crawford said. "But maybe it would be better when there's less chaos!"

"MOM!" George was calling from the hall.

UNDEAD PETS

As Mrs. Crawford went out, Spiker smiled at Erin. "Thanks for not telling."

Erin shrugged. "Want me to help you take the snake home?"

"Sure!" said Spiker. "Have you got a box?"

"Yeah, I think so. There's a shoe box in my room. Come on!"

Joe went to follow them, but just then he heard a small squeak. Flash was sitting on the ledge next to the open window.

"Bye, Joe!"

"What? Are you going already?"

Flash smiled at Joe and a stream of bubbles popped out of his mouth. "Thanks for everything."

And with that, he vanished, leaving nothing but a few bubbles floating around the room.

UNDEAD PETS

"Hey, Joe!" Toby stuck his head into the room. "Doctor Franken-Bubble's about to make square bubbles. Come and see!"

Joe grinned and turned to go when suddenly he heard a strange high-pitched whine coming from behind the armchair.

"Who's there?" Joe said.